BLACK & WHITE

17

۶

۱۹

For all young footballers

BLACK & WHITE

Rob Childs

Illustrated by John Williams

F

FRANCES LINCOLN
CHILDREN'S BOOKS

First published in Great Britain in 2008 by
Frances Lincoln Children's Books,
4 Torriano Mews, Torriano Avenue, London NW5 2RZ

www.franceslincoln.com

British Library Cataloguing in Publication Data
available on request

ISBN: 978-1-84507-751-8

Printed in China

1 3 5 7 9 8 6 4 2

Contents

New Boy

"Right, this way, Joshua. Follow me."

Josh didn't really need any help from the teacher. He heard his new classmates well before he saw them. Their noise gushed out of the open doorway and washed along the school corridor like a tidal wave.

As Mr Blyton led him into the room, the loud conversations subsided and even a minor scuffle in the book corner eventually resolved itself.

"I leave you alone for two minutes and come back to find a mini riot," he remarked. "That's a nice welcome for our new boy, I must say."

Josh felt the full force of thirty pairs of eyes burning into him. He hugged his football against his red tracksuit top, trying to resist the urge to

bounce it on the floor.

"This is Joshua. He's a very keen soccer player, so I'm sure he will soon feel at home here at Westgate."

"You any good?"

The question was shot at Josh by a boy in the front row and was answered by another nearby.

"Good enough to score past you, Raj, I bet."

"Shut up, Anil."

"I expect we'll all find out soon enough just how good he is," said Mr Blyton, showing Josh to a table against the far wall. "Right, Joshua, this is your place next to Matthew. He's going to help you settle in with us."

Matthew responded by scraping his chair a little further away, as if to make more space, but then turned over the page in his book and pretended to be absorbed in the story.

Josh put the ball under the chair and fished into his bag for a book. The picture on the front cover showed a footballer scoring a goal and he made sure that Matthew could see it.

"You know who that is?"

Matthew shook his head.

"Don't you like football?"

Matthew nodded.

"Then you should know his name. He's the best player in Britain."

"This is m..meant to b..be silent reading time," Matthew replied.

Josh shrugged and then banged the book on the table, making the two girls opposite them jump.

Mr Blyton looked their way. "Anything the matter, Joshua?"

"Sorry, just dropped my book," Josh said and held it up in the air.

The teacher peered at the cover. "Isn't that Ossie Williams?"

"He's my uncle!" Josh announced proudly.

"Really? Well I hope that you take after him, Joshua," smiled Mr Blyton. "We could do with some of that Ossie magic in the school team."

At morning break, Matthew started the tour of the school in the playground so that he could eat a packet of crisps.

"Want one?" he said, spluttering a few bits of crisps on to his jumper.

Josh shook his head. "They make you fat."

"Don't care," Matthew shrugged. "I'm hungry."

"Uncle Ossie says footballers have to watch what they eat."

"I *am* watching – all the way into my m..mouth," Matthew grinned, stuffing a few more in to prove it.

"Where's the footie pitch?" asked Josh.

"Ain't got one."

Josh could hardly believe what he'd just heard. "So where do we play our matches?" he demanded.

"On the p..park," Matthew said.

"We had enough space for three pitches at my last school in Wales."

"What you come to this dump for, then?"

Josh sighed. "Parents split up. My mother wanted to move back to the city to be near her own family."

"I ain't got a dad, neither," Matthew confessed. "You get used to it."

Josh changed the subject. "So what's the team like?"

"Rubbish! They ain't won a m..match yet."

"Aren't you in it?"

Matthew gave a shrug. "Can't b..be b..bothered."

"Why not?"

"Dunno really," he began. "Well, some of the kids like to m..make fun of m..me. Y'know..."

Josh nodded, guessing the reason. "You just have to ignore 'em."

"I do."

"Good," Josh said, giving Matthew a grin to show that he was on his side.

"Enid keeps asking m..me to go to one of their p..practices."

"Enid?"

"Enid B..Blyton. That's what we call him."

They both laughed.

"Well, anyway," said Josh, "I'll be going to the next practice, so why don't you come with me?"

"M..might do."

"Right, let's see how good you are," said Josh, taking a tennis ball out of his pocket. "We can have a game with this."

"Rather p..play with that footb..ball of yours."

"Uncle Ossie always played with a tennis ball as a kid. He says if you can control a small ball, it makes a big one dead easy."

Josh flicked the ball up into the air and began to juggle it from foot to foot. Suddenly, he lashed it away on the volley and scored a direct hit. The ball smashed into Matthew's packet of crisps, sending what was left of the contents all over the tarmac. He never even saw it coming.

"Goal!" Josh cried.

Matthew was furious. "I'll get you for that."

Josh sprinted away with Matthew hot on his heels. The chase took them right across the playground, but by the time Matthew caught him up they were both laughing too much to fight.

"Well, at least I've found out how fast you are," Josh panted. "Better to be fit than fat!"

"C'mon, let's go b..back inside and get that b..ball."

"OK, sure – no problem."

But there was a problem, however. When they returned to their places in the classroom, Josh's football had gone.

"Where is it?"

Josh's demand startled the two girls in the far corner of the room. They had been allowed to stay in during break to continue work on their costumes for the Divali celebrations next week.

"Where's what?" said Panna.

"My football."

"How should we know?" said Leela.

"You're the only people in here."

"So?"

"So you might've seen who took it," said Josh, angrily.

Leela stood up to fetch a piece of material from the craft cupboard. "Oh dear! Poor little Joshie has lost his precious ball!" she teased. "What will his famous uncle say?"

Josh pulled a face at her and then stormed out of the room, leaving Matthew trailing in his wake.

"Who was that?" he demanded when Matthew joined him in the corridor.

"Leela. She's OK really – m..most of the time."

Josh stared out of a window across the

playground. "There's my ball!" he cried, pointing.

Matthew looked out and spotted the group of boys kicking the football about. "That's Rajesh and his gang," he groaned. "You've lost it now. You won't get it back off them."

"Just you watch me!" Josh told him. "Come on."

Matthew sighed and reluctantly followed him outside. "Huh! B..bet he wants m..me to do m..more than just watch," he muttered to himself.

By the time Matthew crossed the playground, Josh was already being given the run around by the footballers who were switching the ball between them to keep it out of his reach.

In frustration, Josh launched himself at Rajesh as the gang leader knocked the ball away again and they wrestled each other to the ground.

"Fight! Fight!" cried the other boys and Matthew could not even get close enough to see because of the number of bodies in the way.

He was about to go and fetch the teacher on playground duty when Mr Blyton appeared on the scene, sloshing tea from his mug in his haste.

"Break it up!" he shouted above the noise. "C'mon, finish it – NOW!"

The wrestlers either didn't hear him or chose to ignore the command and Mr Blyton had to step in and separate them himself. His mug ended up the main casualty, smashed to pieces when it dropped to the ground, but both the boys looked a little the worse for wear too. They were breathing raggedly, their clothing dirty and dishevelled, and a few areas of bare skin were scraped and bleeding.

"Inside, you two," Mr Blyton ordered crossly. "Go and get cleaned up. A fine start, Joshua, I must say."

As the teacher escorted them into school to ensure that Round 2 of the fight did not start, Matthew scooped up the stray ball from where it had rolled into a grate and ran off into the building to keep it safe.

Rivals

The playground fight earned Josh instant respect from the other boys, especially as it was agreed that the taller Rajesh had come off worse. He was the school goalkeeper and captain, an honour that Mr Blyton threatened to take away from him if there was any further trouble.

It was not wise to get on the wrong side of Rajesh. He held a grudge against anyone who showed him up in front of his gang – and Josh had gone straight to the top of his hate list.

"B..better watch your b..back, Josh," Matthew warned him. "He'll b..be out to get you."

"Don't worry. I can look after myself," Josh replied.

"Everyb..body knows that now – including Raj," Matthew said with a grin.

Over the next couple of days, however, Rajesh had few opportunities for revenge. Apart from the odd snide remark and sly kick in the corridor, the best he could manage was to tip dirty water over Josh's painting in an art and craft session. Even that backfired. Josh refused to blame him when Mr Blyton asked what had happened, enhancing his reputation further.

Rajesh was not pleased either when Josh joined the group of footballers lining up in the playground to be led round to the nearby park after school for the weekly soccer practice.

"What you doing here?" he snapped.

Josh looked down at his football kit. "Cricket practice?" he suggested with a grin.

Rajesh quelled an outbreak of chuckles from those nearby with a fierce glare.

" Who said you could come?"

"Enid."

"He must be desperate," Rajesh grunted. "He hasn't even seen you play."

"And nor have we," said Anil, one of the team's defenders.

Josh gave a casual shrug. "Well, you soon will."

Mr Blyton arrived on the scene at that point, preventing any further argument.

"Good – all ready?" he said. "Leela?"

Leela checked round the queue to make sure the other four girls in the squad were all there. "Nobody else was in the cloakroom," she said.

"Right, let's go," the teacher told them after counting everybody. "Don't dawdle at the back. Keep up."

Josh had managed to persuade Matthew to come with him to the practice session and Mr Blyton was pleased to see them both there.

"Glad to have you with us at last, Matthew," he said as the children trooped through the park gates. "If you make the team, that left foot of yours will help to give us a better balance. Nobody else is naturally left-footed."

"A good team needs one or two lefties in it," Josh chipped in. "That's what my Uncle Ossie always says."

"So he's left-footed as well, is he?" Matthew remarked.

"How do you know that?" asked Josh.

"Just guessing," said Matthew.

After the usual warm-up period, Mr Blyton had the players practising their ball skills. It was clear how comfortable Josh was, using either foot. He ran at speed with the ball under close control, perfectly balanced and confident.

Not bad – not bad at all, the teacher thought. *Not quite Ossie Williams yet, but you can see the influence.*

He was pleased with Matthew too. In contrast to Josh, Matthew was almost entirely one-footed, but the boy moved well and his passing was crisp and accurate.

Mr Blyton organised the squad into groups for a series of short games against each other, making sure that Josh and Matthew were on the same side. He wanted to see how well they teamed up on the pitch.

He didn't have long to wait. Only a couple of minutes after the start, they linked up along the left touchline, exchanging passes, until Matthew steered a left-footed drive beyond the reach of the sprawling keeper. The goal boosted his confidence, and he created more chances for himself and others.

Only Leela, however, was able to beat the keeper again. She accepted Matthew's pass, jinked her way through two challenges and then slipped the ball past the keeper too.

"Great goal!" praised Matthew, slapping her raised hand in celebration.

"Thanks," she grinned. "Just wanted to show your new pal that girls can play football too. He hasn't passed to me yet."

"He will now, don't worry," Matthew grinned.

Josh made up for his lack of goals in that first match by scoring twice in the next.

Rajesh's team had won both their games, too, and the players had a brief break for drinks before their sides met one another.

"You won't score against me, kid," the goalkeeper boasted, splashing water into Josh's face as he strolled by.

Josh forced himself not to react to the taunt. He

knew his best chance of revenge was on the pitch itself. "We'll see," was all he said.

"We sure will," laughed Rajesh.

Josh was determined to have the last laugh and did everything he could to put the ball past Rajesh. Unfortunately, this worked against the best interests of his own side. He shot at goal from all angles, often with little or no chance of scoring, when a pass to a teammate would have been a better option.

Every time Josh missed, Rajesh laughed at him and even Matthew lost patience.

"Come on, Josh," he complained after another wild attempt. "That's just b..being greedy. Leela was unm..marked there."

Leela wasn't slow to make her own feelings known too – after checking that the teacher could not hear her swear. Josh scowled, knowing that they were right and he was wrong. But Rajesh had got under his skin and he had lost his cool.

"Sorry," he muttered in apology to Matthew. "Just can't help it."

Josh was saved further embarrassment by

Mr Blyton blowing the whistle for the end of the session.

"Ah, well, at least they didn't b..beat us," Matthew said as they pulled on their coats after the goalless draw.

"We should've won, though, and it was my fault," Josh admitted.

Rajesh enjoyed the walk back to school far more than they did. The captain managed to get right behind Matthew and Josh in the line. He put on a false stutter and kept trying to trip them up.

"What a p..p..pity!" Rajesh chortled. "B..b..bet old Uncle Ossie wouldn't have b..b..been b..b..best p..p..pleased. B..b..bet he would've smacked p..p..poor little Joshie's b..b..bottom!"

Welcome Home

"Ma won't be home yet," Josh told Matthew as they left the school building in the fading light after the soccer practice. Neither had bothered to change and had simply pulled a coat over their kit. "Said she was going to see her sister."

Matthew failed to respond in the way that Josh had hoped. He just grunted and slung his bag on to his back.

"Er.. any chance of me coming round to your place for a bit?" Josh prompted. "Y'know, kill a bit of time, like."

Matthew hesitated. "M..my m..mam ain't in, neither. She's at work."

"So? Even better if we've got the place to ourselves."

"She don't like m..me b..bringing anyb..body b..back."

"Why not?"

"She just don't, that's all," Matthew said with a shrug.

"C'mon, Matt," Josh urged. "I won't stay long. She won't even know."

Matthew heaved a sigh. "Well, OK, then."

Josh grinned, pleased with his little victory, and led the way out of the school gate. "Where do you live, anyway? Is it far?"

"Not exactly," Matthew muttered, turning right. "Just a long way up."

"Up?"

"Yeah, up. Tenth floor."

"Wow! Must be a big place."

"Sure is," Matthew replied, nodding towards a block of flats ahead of them. "We're halfway up that thing there."

The lift was out of order, as usual, and the boys trudged up the flights of stairs.

"Sure glad you don't live right at the top," breathed Josh as Matthew fitted his key into the door of the flat.

"Helps to keep m..me fit," Matthew grinned.

Josh chuckled. "Now I know your secret," he said, following Matthew inside. "Any chance of a drink – or oxygen?"

They went into the small kitchen where Matthew poured a couple of glasses of water. The bowl was full of unwashed dishes from breakfast.

"Great view!" Josh exclaimed, gazing out of the window at the twinkling street lights below. "You can see right across the city."

"Yeah, I know," Matthew muttered. "It's a dump."

Josh gave a shrug. "It's just so different to where I used to live, y'know, out in the country. Takes some getting used to."

"M..must do. Do you m..miss it?"

"Well, guess so, a bit.."

"Have you got a b..big house?"

"Nah, just a rented semi," said Josh. "Y'know, till we find a proper place of our own, like."

"You won't b..be leaving Westgate, will you?" Matthew asked. "I m..mean, you've only just got here."

"Nah, you won't get rid of me that easy," Josh said and then grinned. "And nor will Raj. I want to annoy him loads more yet!"

They wandered into the lounge and slumped on to the sofa to watch some cartoons on the television. It was only the sound of the door being slammed that made them realise how dark it had grown.

"Matthew!" came the cry. "Are you in?"

"Yes, M..mam," he stammered, jumping to his feet as his mother came into the lounge and threw on the light.

"Have you been to the shops and..." she began and then stopped when she saw Josh. "Who's this?"

"It's Josh, M..mam – the b..boy I told you ab..bout."

She continued to stare at Josh. "You never told me he was..." Her voice tailed away, but she quickly recovered herself and switched her attention to Matthew. "Just look at the state you're in, boy," she said crossly. "You've got mud all down your legs – and on the sofa. What a mess!"

Josh tried to speak up for Matthew. "Sorry, Mrs..." he began, before realising that he didn't even know Matthew's surname. "It was my idea to..."

She cut him short. "I don't want to hear no excuses from you, neither. My boy knows what's what," she told him. "And for your information, my name's Ms Jones – none of this Mrs business, thank you very much."

She was not best pleased either when she found out that Matthew had not yet done the shopping.

"I left the list and the money in the kitchen as usual. You must have seen it," she raged. "Now get out to them shops before they shut – and take *him* with you."

Josh was very glad to leave and scampered down the flights of stairs.

"Sorry, Matt – didn't mean to get you into any trouble," he said when they reached the bottom and left the building.

"Not your fault," Matthew told him with a shrug. "I should've known b..better."

"Didn't know you had a Welsh surname like mine."

"I don't. Jones is only m..my m..mam's name," he explained. "M..mine's Clarke, like Dad's, b..but he left when I was still a b..baby."

"Do you ever see him?"

"No idea where he is. Could be dead for all I know."

Josh nodded. At least he sometimes saw his own father, who was living near Uncle Ossie, Da's younger brother.

"Anyway," he said, "best get home, I guess. Ma should be back by now. See you tomorrow."

"Sure thing," replied Matthew, setting off

towards the local shops.

Josh received a rather warmer welcome when he let himself in through the back door into his own kitchen, even though Ma frowned at the mud all over his kit.

"Looks like I've got some more washin' to do," she sighed. "And you have, too, young man. Get them dirty things off and then get in that bath. Where's your school things?"

He nodded at the bag that he'd tossed on to the floor. "Oh, my!" she exclaimed, tutting. "They'll be all creased up, somethin' terrible, now."

As he undressed, Josh told her about what had happened at Matthew's.

"Well, you can't blame her," Ma said, as she made him a hot drink to take upstairs. "Just got home from work to find all that mess, poor woman. Bound to be a bit cross. You don't know you're born, young man."

Josh grinned. That was Ma's favourite expression. He disappeared up to the bathroom before Ma could start telling him any tales about what life was like when she was a little girl living in a 'shack', as she always called her family's home on the West Indian island of Barbados.

Even so, he reflected, as he started to run his bath water, Ma was probably right, if Matthew's experience was anything to go by. And then he thought of the massive villa that rich Uncle Ossie now lived in. He didn't even know how many bathrooms that place might have in it.

"One for every day of the week, maybe," he mused, as he lay back to soak in the warm water and sipped his drink. "But, then again, who wants to have a bath every day?"

Team Trials

"Budge up a bit!" Josh complained. "Do you have to take up so much room?"

"Can't help it, can I?" Matthew retorted. "It's just the way I write."

"You're like a crab, the way you hook your arm round like that."

"A lot of left-handed p..people do."

"Why?"

"How should I know? Anyway, you don't m..mind me b..being left-footed – like your Uncle Ossie."

"No, well, that's different," Josh told him. "But you're putting me off, doing all that writing."

"I just like writing stories," Matthew admitted. "I even do them at home sometimes in my b..bedroom."

Josh looked at him in disbelief and shook his head.

Matthew gazed across at Josh's sheet of paper. "Not done m..much yet, have you? Not even half a p..page."

Josh gave a shrug. "I'm stuck."

"Ab..bout what's going to happen next, you m..mean?"

"No – about who's going to play in goal tomorrow."

"What!"

Matthew's exclamation came out louder than intended, causing Mr Blyton to glance up from his desk towards their table.

"Anything the matter over there?" he asked.

Matthew turned bright red, making the girls giggle nearby.

Josh was quick to take the blame. "Sorry, Mr Blyton. Just asking how to spell something," he said. "No problem."

"Good, so on you get now with the story. You can check your spelling later when you redraft it."

Josh groaned quietly. Doing a story once was bad enough, he reckoned. Having to go through it all over again to make changes was even worse.

He much preferred the other task the teacher had given him – choosing a team to play in tomorrow's trial for the local Divali Soccer Sevens tournament at the weekend. He'd already made his choices, but he still had to decide on the players' best positions.

Rajesh was his rival captain, and he had picked a couple of players that Josh would really have liked in his own squad. He fished a crumpled piece of paper from his pocket and looked again at the names. He was still not very happy that the teacher had insisted that both teams were mixed, but at least he had chosen Leela – the best girl – before Rajesh did.

He pushed the paper under Matthew's nose, interrupting him again.

"What d'yer think?" he hissed.

Matthew groaned under his breath. "Ab..bout what?"

"Told you. Who to put in goal?"

"Joe. He did OK last time."

"Yeah, but..."

"Shut up!"

Matthew shoved the paper away and it dropped on the floor. Just as Josh reached down to pick it up, however, Rajesh came by their table and deliberately trod on his hand.

"Aagghh!"

"Who was that?" demanded Mr Blyton.

As eyes turned towards their table, the teacher sighed and went across the room to investigate. Josh was sitting hunched up, his hand between his thighs in an effort to ease the pain.

"What have you done to yourself, Joshua?" said Mr Blyton.

"Just gone and trapped my fingers," he managed to reply through gritted teeth. "Be all right in a minute."

The teacher looked down at Josh's story. "Well,

it's hardly due to writer's cramp, is it, Joshua? I suggest you stay in at break and make some more progress with this."

When Mr Blyton moved away, Matthew leant towards Josh. "Idiot! You should've told him what Raj did," he hissed.

"I don't tell tales," Josh replied, blowing on his fingers. "I'll get him back, don't you worry. Right where it hurts – on the football pitch!"

That was easier said than done, as Josh knew only too well.

★ ★ ★

After the vigorous warm-up session before the start of the trial on the park, Josh gathered his players together for a pep-talk.

"Right, men," he began.

"And girls!" Leela interrupted, winking at her friend, Panna.

Josh shot them a dirty look. "Yeah, and girls," he continued. "Right, if you want to play in the Sevens on Saturday, you need to show Enid how well you can play and..."

Josh carried on talking, but he suddenly became aware that somebody else was standing behind him, listening. Matthew urged him to stop by pretending to cut his own throat, and the other players were trying very hard not to laugh.

Josh turned round and the next few words died on his lips, "...er...sorry..."

"Never mind, Joshua, I've heard that nickname many times before – and worse," Mr Blyton said, failing to hide a smile. "Come on now, let's see some action before everybody gets cold."

That suited Josh fine. He was determined to inspire his team more by how he played than by what he might have said. Even so, when the game began, he was quick to encourage his teammates at every opportunity.

"Good tackle, Brad!...

...Well blocked, Panna!...

...Magic save, Joe!...

...Top shot, Matt!"

The captain's cries echoed around the park and the players responded to the praise by opening

the scoring.

"Great goal, Leela!"

It was Josh's pass that had found Leela with her back to goal, tightly marked by Anil, but she spun past the defender and created enough space to tuck the ball past the diving Rajesh.

"One-nil!" Josh whooped. "Now let's double it."

Rajesh hated letting in goals, and Leela's strike put him in a very bad mood. He roared insults at his defenders for poor marking and moaned at every misplaced pass or wayward shot. He was also much busier himself than he wanted to be, twice having to save shots from Matthew, but he did have the personal satisfaction of turning a fierce drive from Josh wide of the post just before half-time.

"No way you're gonna score, Williams," he muttered as he brushed past Josh on the way towards the teacher.

"We'll see," Josh said with a grin. "Plenty of time left yet."

"Well done, everybody," praised Mr Blyton as the players took long swigs from water bottles to refresh themselves. "There's been some very good football on show. It's going to be difficult to know who to pick for the tournament."

The children looked around at one another, each hoping that they would make the final squad. They knew the score in this game didn't really matter. What was more important was their own performance.

But there were still some personal battles to be won in the second period, none more so than that between the two rival captains. Rajesh took every chance to draw attention to any mistake that Josh made.

"That the best you can do, Williams?" he gloated after Josh had sliced the ball over the bar. "We're not playing rugby, y'know."

Josh made a face at him, but couldn't think of a suitable response in time. And things soon became even worse when Joe let in two quick goals and his team found themselves 2-1 behind.

"We've got 'em now!" bellowed Rajesh. "They won't score again."

He was wrong. The equalizer may have been late, but the quality of the strike made up for that.

It was well worth the wait.

Josh won an important tackle in midfield and the ball ran loose to Leela who looked up to see Matthew sprinting clear down the wing. Her pass was perfect. Matthew took the ball in his stride, steadied himself and then hit a screamer of a shot past a flat-footed Rajesh who barely made a move to stop it.

Mr Blyton beamed in pleasure, amazed at how much more confident Matthew had become since Josh's arrival. It was almost like having two new boys.

With the light fading, he decided this was the ideal moment to call a halt and blew a long blast on the whistle.

"Time to go home," he announced. "I'll pin up the squad for the Sevens on the notice-board tomorrow."

Josh sidled up to him nervously. "Do you know who's going to be in it, Mr Blyton?" he asked, concerned that he might somehow miss out on a place because he hadn't scored.

"Don't worry, Joshua," the teacher reassured

him, seeing the boy's anxious face. He gave him a little wink. "Keep it secret, but your name will be there."

Josh breathed a sigh of relief and went to the side of the pitch to collect his tracksuit top.

"P..pity you didn't p..ut one p..past Raj," Matthew said. "That m..might've shut him up for a b..bit."

"Another time," Josh replied, wishing he could tell his good news. "At least his lot didn't beat us, thanks to you. Bet that goal will clinch your place too."

"Too?"

Josh checked. "Well, you know what I mean. You're bound to be in it."

"Hope so."

"Course – you're our left-hand man!" he grinned. "Hey! I've just come up with a wicked name for our team."

"Oh, yeah – and what's that?"

"Enid Blyton's Secret Seven!"

Fire and Water

"Happy Divali, Josh!" said Leela.

"And the same to you!" Josh grinned.

"Help yourself," she said, offering him a tray of tempting sweets. "They're special Indian sweets. Try one."

Josh took one of the colourful confections from the tray, bit it in half then savoured the taste in his mouth.

"Ooh, they *are* sweet as well," he said, pulling a face. "They must be all sugar."

"Well, that is one of the ingredients," she laughed. "Have another."

"Ta – I will," he said, selecting a red one.

"Matt? You want one?"

Matthew shook his head. "Too sweet for

m..me," he told her.

"Please yourself," she said, turning away. "More for the rest of us."

"Thought you two got on OK usually," Josh said to him. "I mean, you should do. You're our twin strikers tomorrow."

"M..might be. If Enid p..plays us together up front."

"Bound to. He wouldn't have picked you both in the squad otherwise."

The whole school was celebrating Divali, the Festival of Light, whatever the faith of the children – or even if they didn't belong to any religious group at all. This was party time – at least for one afternoon – and there was also to be a big bonfire and fireworks that evening in the park.

"Don't stay up too late," Mr Blyton told his squad of players who had been chosen for the Divali Sevens tournament. "We need you bright and alert on Saturday morning, not half asleep!"

The teacher might well have had his fingers crossed when he said that. He knew that most of the children would not get an early night. Even if they were in bed, the noise of the fireworks would probably keep them awake.

"This is amazing," Josh grinned, gazing at the food and the dozens of divas – the little flickering oil lamps dotted around the classroom. The walls were also covered in colourful rangoli patterns and most of the Hindu children were dressed in bright costumes. "Never seen anything like it before."

"Same every year," Matthew told him. "It's a b..bit like Christmas."

"New to me, anyway. I'm all for it. Better than working."

"Yeah, that's true."

"What d'yer reckon to Divali then, Joshua?" said a voice in his ear.

Josh didn't need to turn round. Only the teachers and the team captain used his full name.

"OK, I guess," he replied, trying to sound cool.

"OK?" Rajesh sneered. "Is that all you can say?"

Josh gave a shrug. "Well, I just said it was amazing, if that'll do."

"Better. And what about p..poor little M..Matthew?" Matthew didn't even bother to respond and moved away instead. "Oh, dear!" Rajesh said with a chuckle. "Your little pal's left you on your own."

"Why did you go and do that?" said Josh. "He can't help having a stammer."

Rajesh shrugged. "Just irritates me, that's all. Like you do."

"Why?"

"Cos you do, that's why, Williams. If it wasn't for losin' the captaincy, I'd have smacked your head in already."

Rajesh gave him a fierce glare and then stalked off.

"Oh, well," Josh sighed. "Now, where did that tray of sweets get to?"

★★★

There were lots of tasty treats on offer that evening in the park, too, with hot dogs and toffee apples for sale alongside more exotic delights.

Josh tried to sample as much of the food as possible, or at least as much as his pocket money or his mother would allow.

"These sweets are delicious, Ma," he said, biting into another. "You should try one."

"No, thanks – I'm just here to watch the fireworks," she said and then smiled. "And to keep an eye on you, young man. Don't want you wanderin' off in the dark."

"No need to worry. I've got lots of new mates

here."

"That's as maybe – but you can never be too careful," she said. "Remember what I've told you. City folks are different to what you've been used to back in Wales." Josh grinned, knowing exactly what was coming next. "Now when I was a little gal on the island..."

A huge bang made them both jump and saved Josh from yet another story about how life used to be so much simpler back in 'the old days'. The firework display had started and they stood mesmerised by all the noise and flashing lights which kept exploding across the black sky.

"Now they's what I call real fireworks," laughed his mother in delight. "Last time I saw anythin' like them was at that big party in Ossie's garden. Remember that, Josh?"

He was hardly likely to forget what happened that night. It was when his father told Ma that he was leaving her.

As another rocket exploded into a cascade of coloured, sparkling lights, somebody lurched past them, almost knocking his mother over.

"Hey! My bag!" she screamed. "He's took my bag!"

Josh whirled round in time to see the hooded bag-snatcher pushing his way through the crowd.

"Stop him!" he yelled at the top of his voice, but it was too late for anybody to react.

Josh gave chase himself, darting through gaps in the groups of people and almost knocking over a younger child.

Josh scurried this way and that, getting the occasional glimpse of someone else running away ahead of him. It was only when he broke free of the crowd, however, that he managed to get a better view. The black sky was again illuminated by a shower of lights and Josh saw him heading for a small wood near the lake.

As Josh sprinted in pursuit, there was something about the way the thief ran that reminded him of somebody, but he couldn't think clearly. One thing he did know for sure was that he was gaining on him.

Perhaps the thief thought that, too, for he disappeared into the trees. Josh decided to skirt the wood, hoping to cut off any escape route towards the park gates, but the figure emerged on the far side and made for the lake instead.

Josh was not far behind by the time they reached the water's edge where they both halted, panting. He was unsure now just what to do. Although the thief wasn't that much bigger than him, Josh didn't know whether he might even be carrying a knife and so kept his distance.

"You've got my mother's bag!" he cried. "Give it back." The hood was suddenly thrown back to reveal a familiar face. "Rajesh!"

"Dead right, wonder-boy! You want it – you fetch it," he taunted. "But you're gonna have to swim for it!"

As Rajesh swung the bag round and hurled it into the lake, Josh hurtled down the slope towards him. His momentum was such that he couldn't stop and Rajesh was too slow to dodge out of his way. Josh grabbed hold of his arm and both of them ended up toppling full-length into the cold water, splashing and floundering in the shallows to try and find their feet.

Fortunately, the lake was not very deep, even in the middle, and Josh began to wade further out, his progress hampered by the thick mud at the bottom. He had lost all interest in Rajesh, for the time being, and was intent upon his search for the bag.

Rajesh had managed to clamber out on to the bank, cursing Josh.

"These are my new jeans for Divali!" he wailed. "And my new trainers!"

"Good," Josh retorted. "I hope they're not waterproof."

Josh was lucky that the bag had not sunk out of sight into the mud. The strap had snagged on a floating branch and he was able to reach forward, now almost waist-deep in the water, to grab hold of it.

As Josh turned in triumph, Rajesh decided to make himself scarce and had disappeared through the gates by the time Josh squelched back up on to dry land, shivering, to be greeted by his frantic mother.

"Got it back, Ma!" he grinned, handing over the

filthy, water-logged bag.

"Oh, you silly boy!" she cried, hugging him in relief, despite the muddy state that he was in. "You could've gone and got yourself drowned!"

"I'm OK, Ma. Don't worry."

"C'mon – home with you, young man," she ordered, taking him by the arm. "You're goin' straight in that bath."

Josh wasn't sure he really saw the point of that. He'd already just had one. But at least the water at home would be nice and hot.

Group Games

"Who are you?"

Matthew was taken by surprise when a slim woman opened the front door of Josh's house. He had rather expected Josh to come bursting out. Brad's father was giving them both a lift to the tournament.

"Er, I'm M..Matt," he faltered. "Josh's m..mate at school."

"Look, Josh won't be comin'," she said. "He's got a cold startin' and I'm keepin' him inside."

Matthew hardly knew what to say. "B..but we're p..playing in the Sevens..."

"Well, you might be, but not my Josh. He's stayin' right here in the warm."

"Ma!" came a cry. "Is that Matt?"

Matthew looked past her to see Josh come dashing down the stairs, wearing blue pyjamas instead of the school's black and white stripes.

"Ma! I've got to go," he pleaded. "They need me."

"Well, they'll just have to do without you today," she told him and then turned back to Matthew. "I'm sorry, but like I said, he can't go. Goodbye!"

The door closed and Matthew was left standing on the path, listening to Josh's howls of protest and the woman telling him to go back to bed.

He trudged back up the garden path to where the car was parked and reported what had happened.

"Oh, great!" Brad muttered. "Without Josh, we've got no chance."

"C'mon, then," said Brad's father. "Let's get to the school and report the bad news to your teacher."

★★★

By the time the team arrived at the venue for the

Sevens, they were running late because of roadworks, and they found that their first group match was due to start. The players did not even have a chance to warm up properly.

The captain, however, was secretly relieved about Josh's absence. Rajesh hadn't really fancied having to face up to him after what had happened last night. "Don't matter that Josh ain't here," Rajesh sneered. "We don't need him."

Most of the others did not share that opinion and they soon found themselves in trouble. Another lad, Jay, took Josh's place in midfield, but it was his stray pass that led to Westgate falling behind after only two minutes.

"Sort it out!" roared Rajesh, angrily kicking the ball back upfield for the re-start. "Where was the marking?"

No one dared point out to the goalkeeper that he might have made a better effort to save the shot after the ball had slithered beneath his body into the net.

Things went from bad to worse after that and the team slumped to a 3-0 defeat, barely managing a shot at goal. Their opponents, Cranfield Juniors, were simply too strong and looked to be favourites to win the tournament, especially when they beat the other school in the group by an even bigger margin.

"There's still a chance for us to make the semi-finals," said Mr Blyton. "If we don't lose the next game, we can qualify on goal-difference. A draw would be enough."

Even that was going to be difficult after Westgate again conceded an early goal. They were still losing, despite an equalizer from Leela before half-time, when a man came up to speak to Mr Blyton.

"What's the score?"

"Two-one to them," said the teacher glumly. "Looks like we might be going home early."

"I've only just got here," the man replied. "Where's my Josh?"

"Josh? Are you his father?"

He nodded. "Sure am. He don't know his da come all the way from Wales to see him play."

"Well, I'm afraid your journey might have been wasted, Mr Williams."

Mr Blyton explained the situation and the man's face creased up in annoyance.

"That woman!" he grumbled. "My boy should be here."

"We're certainly missing him," admitted Mr Blyton, who then almost missed something himself. He turned his attention back to the game just in time to see Matthew stab home a pass from Leela to bring the scores back level.

"Well done!" he called out. "Concentrate. Don't let them score again."

When Mr Blyton looked round to continue his conversation, he found that he was now standing by himself. Mr Williams was striding away across the playing field towards the car park.

Oh, dear! the teacher sighed. *I do hope I haven't gone and put my foot in it.*

There was nothing he could do about that now – and nor could he do much about what was happening on the pitch. They had a chance to win the game, which Matthew wasted by ballooning the ball over the bar, and then they almost lost it when a slip by Anil allowed his opponent a clear sight of goal. Only Rajesh's acrobatic leap saved them as he turned the ball around a post for a corner.

The referee's whistle sounded before the kick could even be taken, leaving the scores level at 2-2.

"We're through!" screamed Panna.

"Don't get too excited," growled Rajesh. "It's only the semis next, not the Final – and we ain't gonna win that, the way you lot are playing."

There was a short break before the semi-final matches and Mr Blyton told the children to put their coats on, have a drink of water and try to keep warm.

"Who are we playing in the semis?" asked Brad's father.

"The team that won the other group," said Mr Blyton. "And they look pretty good from what I've seen of them."

"Pity Josh isn't here."

Mr Blyton nodded. "It certainly is," he murmured, wondering whether the boy might yet appear.

★★★

As Westgate kicked off their semi-final, however, Mr Williams was still arguing with his ex-wife and demanding that Josh get his kit on. Only with the greatest reluctance did she agree to let their son play – and then only on the condition that he was brought straight back home afterwards.

By the time Mr Williams had bundled Josh into the car and managed to get through the roadworks again, the match was already over. Josh dashed from the car park towards where he spotted his teammates grouped around Mr Blyton.

"Look! It's Josh!" cried Leela.

"Sorry!" he shouted. "Hope I'm not too late."

Rajesh ran forward to meet him. "What for?" the captain demanded.

"To play," said Josh. "We're still in it, aren't we?"

"Less of the *we*, kid," Rajesh sneered. "You can't even bother to turn up."

"Well, we both know why I've got this cold, don't we?" retorted Josh. "After what you did last night."

"Have you told anybody?"

"Course not."

"Good job too," Rajesh retorted. "Or you'd be dead!"

Josh ignored the threat. "My da said we were struggling."

"Did he, now? Well you can tell him we're in the Final – no thanks to you."

The rest of the team surrounded them, bubbling with excitement.

"We won one-nil..."

"Raj was brill..."

"Brad got the winner..."

"First goal I've scored all season..."

"Glad to see you, Joshua," Mr Blyton smiled. "Are you fit enough to play?"

"Sure am!" Josh grinned, opening his coat to reveal his kit. "Can't wait."

"You won't have to," the teacher told him. "We're on again soon."

Final Touch

"Shoot!"

Leela shot. She was going to, anyway, no matter what Josh might have shouted when he passed to her. The ball beat the diving goalkeeper but struck the foot of the post and rebounded to safety.

"Bad luck!" Josh cried. "It'll go in next time."

Leela shook her head and sighed. She knew there might not even be a 'next time'. The team had barely managed a single shot against Cranfield Juniors in the group game and needed an early goal in the Final to boost their confidence.

Josh, however, had not played in that match and treated the Juniors as just another team. "C'mon, men!" he demanded as if he were the captain. "We can beat this lot."

Leela did not bother to remind him this time about the fact there were two girls in the side, but his cries did not go unnoticed by the opposition

"Who's the mouthy kid?" asked one of the Juniors who was marking Matthew. "Didn't see him before."

"He's our secret weapon," he grinned. "We were just saving him for the Final."

"Huh! You've still got no chance against us."

Josh had attracted the attention of Cranfield's teacher too. He wandered up to Mr Blyton on the touchline and put the same query more politely. "Who's the lad wearing the number four shirt? He looks quite useful."

"You might know his uncle better," chuckled Mr Blyton.

"Oh, yes? And who's that?"

"Ossie Williams!"

The man's jaw dropped open. "Really!" he gasped. "Where have you been hiding him all morning?"

Mr Blyton smiled. "It's a long story. I'm just glad he's here now."

His teammates felt exactly the same way. Even Rajesh had to admit that Josh now gave them a better chance of success.

But the Juniors were still strong favourites to win the trophy and were determined to do so. They mounted a series of raids and only failed to score because of good defending and a remarkable save by Rajesh. The on-form keeper was wrong-footed by a deflection, but somehow managed to block the ball with his trailing leg.

"Mark tight!" he demanded. "Don't give 'em so much room."

It was almost inevitable that all this pressure would lead to a goal, which it did just before the interval, but Westgate were performing much better than they had done in their first encounter with the Juniors.

"Keep this up!" Mr Blyton encouraged the players during the short break. "Try to get the ball to Josh as much as possible. He's fresher than anyone else on the pitch, even if he's not fully fit."

It was true, Josh was feeling the effects of his cold, but he took inspiration from the fact that his dad was watching him play.

"C'mon, my boy!" bellowed Mr Williams as the teams lined up again for the second half. "You show 'em how Ossie would do it!"

Cranfield's teacher had also warned his players about who Josh was, but that had perhaps only served to make them a little more nervous and wary of him when he had the ball at his feet. They gave him too much respect, and certainly too much space. And it wasn't long before he made them pay the price.

Receiving the ball just inside his own half of the pitch, Josh moved forward, looking for a striped shirt to pass to. Instead, he found the opposition backing off, allowing him to advance deep into their territory.

Josh wasn't one to refuse an opportunity to shoot. As soon as he had a clear sight of goal, Josh let fly with his right foot and the ball was bouncing back from the net before the keeper had time to react. The poor boy only caught hold of the ball on its way out.

"What a goal!" screamed Mr Williams as Josh

was mobbed by his celebrating teammates. "You beauty!"

To their credit, the Juniors recovered from the shock of conceding the equalizer and hit back with more attacks of their own. Time and again, the favourites went close to restoring their lead but could not find a way past Rajesh again.

The captain was having the game of his life, perhaps spurred on by the desire to outdo his rival. The goalkeeper pulled off a number of fine saves, the best of which had all the spectators applauding.

The Juniors simply could not believe they had failed to score. Rajesh had dived full length to turn the first shot against a post and then had somehow recovered in time to block the rebound at point-blank range.

"Great stuff, Raj!" cried Josh generously. "Fantastic!"

Rajesh grinned as teammates came up to slap their keeper on the back.

"Right, I've done my stuff," he told them. "Now you go and do yours at the other end."

Josh did exactly that. With time running out –

and the prospect of a penalty shoot-out to find a winner – Josh started a rare Westgate raid by sweeping the ball out to Matthew near the touchline.

"Take him on, Matt," he cried. "Beat him for speed."

His opponent found out just how fast Matthew was. The striker pushed the ball past him and sprinted after it, leaving the defender for dead. The ball almost went dead, too, but Matthew just managed to catch it up before it ran out of play. He looked up to see Leela's waving arm, signalling where she wanted the ball.

The cross was perfect, right into her path, but both her marker and the goalkeeper had closed in to make any shot very difficult. Leela didn't even bother touching the ball. She suddenly let it zip past her, selling them a dummy, and the ball rolled invitingly across the deserted area.

The only player who could reach it was Josh. He had continued his lung-bursting run forward, outpacing any defender, and now he stretched out a leg in a desperate attempt to make contact with the ball.

He did so – just. The ball hit his shin rather than his boot, but it was enough to send it bouncing into the unguarded net to put Westgate 2-1 ahead.

Josh was almost too weary to stand up by himself and he was hauled to his feet by teammates. Exhausted by the effects of the cold, he was in no fit state to carry on and Mr Blyton replaced him with Jay for the last two minutes of the game.

"That's my boy!" cried his father, giving him a big bear hug on the touchline. "Pity your ma ain't here to see what you done."

Josh wished his mother had come, too, but right now he was simply hoping and praying that the team could hold on to their precious lead. When the final whistle sounded, Josh leapt into the air in relief, forgetting his tiredness, and raced on to the pitch to join in the celebrations.

He even shook hands with Rajesh. "Let's forget what happened before," Josh suggested. "Friends?"

Rajesh gave a shrug. "Maybe," he replied. "For now, anyway."

Rajesh soon stepped forward to receive the trophy, along with his individual medal. The rest of the squad followed to receive theirs, too, each showing a Divali garland with a little diva lamp glowing inside it.

"Champions!" cried Mr Williams as the players posed for photographs.

It made them all laugh and provided an excellent picture for the local newspaper.

Westgate's success had indeed been a real team effort, but it had needed their star player, Josh, to provide the magic final touch.

On the Run

No one saw Josh at school the following week. He was kept at home to recover from his cold and so he was delighted when Matthew turned up on his doorstep at the weekend.

"Thought I'd b..best come round to see how you are."

"OK now, pretty much," Josh said and then grinned. "A week off school does anybody good!"

"Yeah, guess so," Matthew replied. "You fit enough for a b..bit of a kickab..bout on the p..park?"

"Sure," he said, looking round quickly to check his mother wasn't listening, in case she disagreed. "Just give me a minute to get my trainers."

"And a b..ball!"

"Yeah, right."

Josh reappeared in less than a minute, his trainers still untied.

"Let's go," he urged, tossing a football to Matthew and closing the front door quietly. "Before Ma finds out!"

They set out for the park on the trot, tapping the ball between them until Josh tripped over his own laces.

"Hold on!" he cried, kneeling down. "Let me do these up."

"That happened to m..me during cross country this week," Matthew told him. "Nearly lost m..my shoe in the m..mud near the lake."

"Cross country?"

"Well, just round the p..park, like. We always do some running this time of year. Enid reckons it helps us keep fit over the winter. C'mon, race you to the p..park!"

Josh hadn't even finished tying his laces. "Hey! Wait for me!" he cried as Matthew set off. "That's not fair."

He almost caught Matthew up at the traffic lights, but Matthew still beat him to the park gates.

"The winner!" cried Matthew, laughing.

"Huh!" Josh panted. "Only cos of my cold. And I was carrying the ball."

"Looks like you'll have to do some training if you want to m..make the team," Matthew grinned.

"What team?"

"For the Area Championships," Matthew told him. "I came tenth last year in m..my age group."

"Tenth? Is that all?"

"Well, it's not too b..bad. There were over a hundred runners."

"Fair enough," Josh conceded.

He kicked the ball on to the grass and sprinted after it. "C'mon, slowcoach!" he laughed, catching Matthew off guard. "We can practise our footie and running at the same time."

They had a lively, boisterous game together over

the next half an hour. They hardly noticed how messy their clothes had become until they stopped and sat on a bench for a rest.

"Look at m..my jeans!" moaned Matthew, examining the mud stains all down one side. "M..mam'll do her nut."

"Ma won't be best pleased, neither," admitted Josh, pulling a face. "She don't even know where I went."

"C'mon, let's get b..back," said Matthew, standing up. "It'll b..be dark soon."

They reached Josh's house first and parted at the garden gate.

"Good luck!" said Matthew.

"And you."

"Yeah, I'll need it," he grunted. "See you at school next wcek – if we're b..both still alive!"

★★★

"Take it nice and steady at the start," Mr Blyton told the runners. "Don't charge off too quickly. Just go at your own pace."

The teacher always gave the same sort of advice before any training run, but he suspected that this time his words might fall on deaf ears. The children knew that a good performance would earn them a place in the school squad for the Area Championships.

Mr Blyton set them off and Josh immediately surged into the lead, well ahead of the main pack. He felt back to full fitness and wanted to prove it to everyone, including the teacher.

Over the past fortnight, Josh had been doing secret training sessions on his own around the park and knew the course very well. They needed to cover the perimeter of the park twice, plus an extra circuit of the lake, and Josh was setting a hot pace out in front.

"Not so fast, Joshua," Mr Blyton called out to him. He wasn't sure whether the boy had heard him or not, for Josh showed no sign of slowing down. The lead, if anything, was increasing, and no one else seemed willing to try and close the gap. Most of the others were still bunched up, running shoulder to shoulder, with Matthew almost jogging

along and keeping plenty of energy in reserve for the later stages.

On the second lap of the course, over on the far side of the park, Matthew put in a little burst of speed to overtake a number of runners. He was feeling comfortable and confident, and had Josh in his sights, when all of a sudden his world turned upside down. He had been tripped from behind and hit the ground so hard that all the breath was knocked from his body.

"You OK, Matt?" someone asked, pausing briefly to check.

Leela was standing over him as he knelt up and nodded. "Yeah - thanks - you carry on," he gasped.

Most of the runners had surged past him by the time Matthew got groggily back to his feet. He began to stumble forward, determined to continue, but it took a while for him to find his usual rhythm.

Meanwhile, out in front, a tiring Josh glanced over his shoulder to see that some people were not too far behind. His legs felt heavier and his breathing became more ragged. "C'mon!" he urged himself. "Keep going!"

He was on a downward slope and was able to coast for a short distance until he felt more comfortable. But his lead had now been cut considerably and the chasers were closing in.

Josh saw Mr Blyton ahead of them, signalling for the runners to turn right and go round the lake.

"Keep it up!" cried the teacher to all of them as they passed him. "Not far to go now."

It was still far enough, however, for plenty of places to change as some of the children faded and others found a late surge of energy. Mr Blyton stayed there long enough to ensure that even the backmarkers knew which course to take and then he jogged away towards the finishing area.

The mud around the lake took its toll upon many weary legs and some children were reduced to walking part of the way. From experience, Josh knew how to avoid the worst areas, but the nearest chasers followed him and there was nothing he could do to prevent two of them from overtaking him.

"Got you – at last!" gasped Joe.

Anil didn't say a word, but the smirk on his face

forced Josh to keep going. Somehow, he managed to stay close behind Anil as the leading trio rounded the eastern edge of the lake and made for the finish.

Matthew would normally have expected to be up at the front, too, but because of his fall he was some way behind. Overtaking some runners, he heard a familiar voice.

"Enjoy your trip?"

Matthew suspected it might have been Raj who tripped him up and he was sorely tempted to give him a dose of his own medicine. With difficulty, he resisted barging into him and ran on instead.

"B..best revenge is to b..beat him," he muttered to himself.

There was certainly no way that Rajesh was going to catch Matthew now, and the same was true for Josh as far as the frontrunner, Joe, was concerned. But Anil was another matter entirely. Anil had been mentally unprepared for Josh to come back at him and could not respond when, with the finish in sight, Josh pounded past him into second place.

They were the first three boys' names written in Mr Blyton's notebook, half of the team of six needed for the Area Championships. Those did not include Matthew, who could only finish eighth, just behind the first girl, Leela.

"Bad luck, Matt," Josh said, knowing that Matthew would only be picked as reserve. "I was expecting you to catch me up."

"Yeah, m..might've done, if I hadn't b..been tripped," he scowled.

Josh was angry when he heard what Rajesh had done and tried to persuade Matthew to tell Mr Blyton what had happened.

Matthew shook his head. "Too late now – and, anyway, I've got no p..proof. Raj would only deny it."

Josh sighed in frustration. "So that bully-boy

gets away with it again. One of these days..."

"What?"

"I don't know yet," Josh said with a grimace. "But one of these days he's really got it coming to him. I'll see to that."

Touch and Go

As winners of the Divali tournament, Westgate had been invited to take part in the annual County Sevens. It was an honour for the school and the soccer practices were now being used to prepare the squad and work on their tactics.

"Touch and go!" cried Mr Blyton.

The players were training in small groups in the ten-metre square grids that had been marked out on the park. The teacher wanted to improve their quick-passing skills, allowing them only one or two touches before moving into new positions to get the ball back.

"Give it and go!" shouted Mr Blyton.

Josh gave it and went, picking up Matthew's return pass and then knocking the ball on to Leela.

They were playing three against one and were giving Jay the run-around. The trio's movement and inter-passing was so good that he just couldn't get the ball off any of them.

"Come on!" Jay moaned. "Give me a chance."

Leela flicked the ball away from him towards Matthew and laughed. She, too, had been 'piggy-in-the-middle' and knew how it felt.

"Up to you, Jay," she giggled. "Go and get it!"

Jay expected the ball to be switched to Josh, but Matthew wrong-footed him by sliding it back to Leela. Jay was becoming more and more frustrated and when Leela underhit her next pass to Josh, Jay seized his chance. He and Josh both met the ball at the same time, but Jay's boot also made contact with Josh's left ankle.

Josh yelped in pain and hobbled a few metres before crumpling to the ground.

"Sorry Josh," Jay apologised. "Didn't mean to hurt you."

"Save those sorts of tackles for the opposition, not for teammates," Leela told him crossly.

"I said I'm sorry," Jay retorted. "I was just fed

up chasing the ball."

"Still no need to go crunching in like that."

Matthew bent over Josh in concern. "How's it feel?"

"Sore," Josh grunted.

Mr Blyton pressed gently on the boy's ankle, making him wince.

"Let's see if you can stand up, Joshua," he said, holding his arm in support. "Take your weight on the other foot at first."

Balancing on one leg, Josh gingerly put his left foot to the ground and then immediately pulled it back up.

"Right, go and sit over there on the bench and rest for a while," the teacher told him. "Help him, please, Matthew."

"How b..bad is it?" said Matthew when they reached the bench.

Josh yanked off his boot and rolled down his

sock, spilling the shin pad on to the grass. There was a long red graze across his ankle bone.

"Bad enough," he said, rubbing it gingerly. "But I'll live."

"Good – so I'll leave you here to suffer," Matthew smiled. "I want to get b..back into the action."

Leela was a little more sympathetic. "You'll need some cream and a plaster on that," she said. "It's bleeding a bit."

"You can kiss it better, if you like," Josh grinned.

"You've got to be joking!" she retorted. "Not with your smelly feet!"

As the practice session carried on without him, Josh stood up a couple of times, but he still found it too painful to walk.

"Don't much fancy hopping all the way back to school," he muttered.

He wasn't very keen on the alternative either, but when the session ended, Mr Blyton gave him no choice. Much to Josh's embarrassment, and to the great amusement of the other players, he was given a lift, piggyback-style, through the streets on the teacher's back.

It was only the following day that it became clear that Josh's injury was no laughing matter. He hobbled into the school playground, his left ankle tightly strapped for support.

"Ma reckons I've twisted it or something," he told Matthew as the bell rang. "It's still really stiff and sore."

"B..but what ab..bout the Area cross country?"

"Bad news for me, I guess, but good news for somebody else."

"Who?"

"You! You're reserve."

The penny suddenly dropped. Matthew had been too concerned about Josh to realise what the injury might mean for himself.

"Oh, yes – right," he murmured. "Well, I hope so. I m..mean, if you can't m..make it, like."

"C'mon, let's go and tell Enid."

Rajesh and Anil blocked their path into the school building.

"Here he comes!" Rajesh sneered. "The wounded hero!"

"No way you're goin' to be runnin' on Sat'day," Anil said, looking at the ankle strapping and sniggering.

"Dead right, Anil," Josh replied, then grinned. "But Matt will be now – and he'll beat you, too, just like I did. Cos Raj won't be there this time to trip him up again."

"Never touched him!" Rajesh snorted, but gave away the lie with a smirk.

That was all the proof Josh needed. Rajesh did not even see the punch coming, but he certainly felt it. Josh's right fist smacked into his face and Rajesh sprawled on the ground, too stunned to get up again and try to hit back.

Anil was in no position to help either. As he made to move forward, Matthew grabbed hold of him from behind, pinning his arms to his side.

"Got anything else to say?" Josh demanded,

standing over Rajesh who made a feeble attempt to kick out at Josh's bandaged foot. "No? Didn't think so. C'mon, Matt, let's go in."

Matthew pushed Anil roughly away and followed Josh into the school. "Wicked p..punch!" he grinned. "Thanks – b..but I can fight m..my own b..battles, y'know."

"Sure you can," Josh agreed, opening and closing his right hand to ease the ache. "But I don't reckon either of us will be having any more bother from him."

It had happened so quickly that hardly anyone else witnessed the playground drama. But there had been at least one spectator. Passing a second-floor window inside the school, Mr Blyton had spotted Josh's arrival and paused to see how the boy was walking. He also saw more of the punch than Rajesh.

Right, it's about time I took some action, he decided and went down the stairs towards his classroom.

Leela had already told him about Matthew's trip during the race – and also who had done it. She wasn't normally one to tell tales but she felt on this occasion that it was justified. She was fed up of Rajesh and his gang throwing their weight around.

"Good morning, lads," the teacher greeted them when he met Josh and Matthew in the corridor. "An interesting way to start the day, I see."

The boys glanced at each other.

"How do you mean, Mr Blyton?" said Josh, trying to look innocent.

"Are you thinking of taking up boxing as well, Joshua?"

Josh gave up the pretence and looked guilty instead.

"I don't believe that's the right way to settle arguments," said the teacher.

"Sorry, sir," Josh mumbled.

"I know what was behind all that nonsense in the playground so we'll say no more about it – as long as that's the end of it," Mr Blyton said sternly.

Joshua nodded.

"Good," said the teacher and then turned to Matthew. "Joshua is clearly unfit to run in the Area

Championships, so you will take his place. It seems that you deserve to be in the team, anyway, Matthew, and I'm sure you'll do well."

Mr Blyton spoke to Rajesh in private, warning him about his future behaviour. He also carried out his previous threat and stripped Rajesh of the soccer captaincy, which reduced the goalkeeper to tears.

"I'm sorry, Rajesh, but it has to be done, for the sake of the team. I can't have the captain behaving like you have done."

"But Josh thumped me!"

"Yes, and he knows that was wrong too. It won't happen again."

★ ★ ★

On the next Saturday morning Matthew ran the race of his life.

It was a hilly course, but he was extra determined to do well – for himself, for the team and for his friend. He suspected that Josh was perhaps not as badly injured as it seemed, especially when Josh kept popping up at several different

vantage points to cheer him on. Gone, too, he noticed, was the strapping on his foot.

Another incentive for him was the fact that his mother was watching.

Matthew had been amazed – and delighted – by her sudden decision to travel to the Championships with the party from the school

"Are you sure you want to go, M..mam?" he said. "I m..mean, it's not like a football m..match. Just a load of kids running around."

"That's all football is to me, too, boy," she told him and then smiled. "I just want to see how good you really are."

His mother cheered and clapped as she watched Matthew go by on the second circuit of the course, well placed behind the leading group.

"Go on, Matthew!" she screamed. "You show 'em, boy!"

Matthew heard her voice and it spurred him on even more. He tackled the uphill sections with great spirit and energy, overtaking anyone who was beginning to flag. He'd already left Westgate's other best runners, Joe and Anil, well behind.

"You can do it, Matt!" cried Josh as the leaders splashed through a muddy patch. "Keep it up!"

Matthew flashed him a mud-stained grin and was gone.

In the end, despite a lung-bursting sprint towards the finishing-line, he wasn't quite able to catch the front two, but Matthew was good enough to claim third place and earn his mother's congratulations.

"Well done, boy!" she praised him when he showed his medal to her after the presentation ceremony. "I'm real proud of you!"

County Cup

"Great save, Joe!" cried Brad, the new Westgate captain. "Magic!"

The goalkeeper was new too. Joe picked himself up and grinned. His performances in the cross country had given him more confidence, which had been boosted further by his selection for the County Cup tournament.

Rajesh had decided not to play for the school any more. The loss of the captaincy was a big blow to his self-esteem and his reputation, making him even more surly.

"You won't stand a chance without me in goal," he told the other footballers. "I was the star at Divali."

"Yeah, till Josh turned up," Anil retorted.

"Huh! It was only my saves that kept us in it."

Rajesh had wanted Anil to desert the school team, too, and play just for their Sunday League club, but Anil had refused, much to Rajesh's fury. It seemed that he could not even tell members of his old gang what to do now.

The former captain had not travelled with them into the city to the County Ground to watch the Sevens, much to everyone else's relief. They were not missing him. Joe had been outstanding in their group games, one of the main reasons that they had qualified for the semi-finals.

Another star of the team was Leela, who had scored in every match. She had not managed to do so yet in this one, but went close in their next attack. Her shot eluded the keeper's dive, but the ball bobbled just wide of the target.

"Bad luck!" called out Brad from his position in the middle of the defence, clapping his hands in encouragement. "So close!"

"Next one will go in," shouted Brad's father in support. "You'll see."

He was right – and wrong. Unfortunately, the

ball went in their own net instead, with Joe beaten for only the second time that morning.

"Oh, dear!" sighed Mr Blyton. "We're in trouble now."

The players' parents were equally worried. There was a big crowd for this important occasion – including one man on the touchline that not even his own son would have recognized.

"What the hell are you doing here?" demanded Matthew's mother.

Her ex-husband whirled round at the sound of her voice.

"Might ask you the same question," he said with a smirk. "You were never a sports fan."

"I am now – of *my* son's sports," she retorted.

"Well, that's why I'm here too," he told her. "I saw his name and picture in the paper after the cross-country, rang up the school and found out about this tournament.

"They had no right to tell you."

"Maybe not, but I'm glad they did," he grinned. "Didn't know Matt was so talented."

"Well that just proves he don't take after you, then!" she snapped and stalked off round the pitch to stand well way from him.

The half-time whistle had blown for drinks of water and to allow the teachers a chance to give their players a few words of encouragement.

"It's only one-nil," said Mr Blyton. "No need to panic. Just keep playing the way you have all morning and we can still win this game."

Although Josh seemed his usual self and had scored even more goals than Leela, the teacher kept checking to make sure the boy was in no pain.

"How's the ankle, Joshua?"

He received the same simple answer as before.

"OK."

Mr Blyton smiled. He knew that the next thing he said would have a far more enthusiastic response. "Good – because someone has just arrived who I'm sure would love to see you at your best."

"Who's that?"

"Ossie Williams!"

"Uncle Ossie!" Josh cried. "Where?"

The teacher pointed towards the changing rooms where the tables were already set up for the later presentation of the trophy and medals. Josh saw his dad first and then spotted Uncle Ossie surrounded by a group of autograph hunters.

"Da! Uncle!" he shouted in excitement.

They both waved back to him, but there was no time to talk. The referee was waiting to get the second half underway.

Inspired by their presence, Josh turned on some of that 'Ossie Magic', just as Mr Blyton hoped. He demanded the ball at every opportunity to show off all his skills.

"That's the way, Joshie-Boy!" cried Ossie, who was now on the touch-line.

The star's presence seemed to affect the other team, too. Whenever Josh had the ball, they seemed to freeze, unsure what to do, allowing him as much

time and space as he needed.

He set up the equalizer by cleverly back-heeling the ball to the unmarked Anil, who had moved upfield to support an attack, and the defender lashed in his first goal of the season.

Matthew was the next to benefit from Josh's skills. The striker sprinted past his marker to receive his friend's perfectly weighted pass, taking it in his stride and shooting firmly past a helpless goalkeeper to put Westgate 2-1 ahead.

"Good goal, Matthew!" cried his mother.

"That's my boy!" shouted his father, shaking his fists in the air in delight.

Josh ran up to Matthew and ruffled his hair. "Who's that guy over there, doing his nut?"

Matthew glanced across to the touch-line and then shook his head. "No idea. Never seen him b..before."

"Well he seems to know you all right."

Matthew gave a shrug. " Let's just get on with the game."

The result was no longer in doubt. Time soon ran out and the referee blew his whistle to confirm

Westgate's victory.

"Put your coats on and keep warm," Mr Blyton told his players. "There will be a bit of time to wait yet before the Final, but don't go wandering off."

Josh ran over to greet his dad and uncle. "I didn't even know you'd be here," he grinned.

"Sure glad we made it in time," said Da. "We got lost!"

Ossie laughed. "You were the one readin' the map, man. Nearly missed seein' Joshie-Boy run rings round all them other kids!"

"What about United?"

"Oh, we're not playin' till tomorrow, Joshie-Boy. Boss gave us the day off."

"Ossie's already been nabbed," Da chuckled.

"How d'you mean?" asked Josh.

"Soon as we turned up, he got asked if he'd present the cup," Da told him. "You'll have to win it now so he can give it to you!"

"I'm not the skipper, Da," Josh reminded him.

"Yeah, well, you and Ossie can still have your picture took with the cup for the papers."

Matthew was also having his own family

reunion, but this one wasn't so pleasant.

"Well played, son," said the man who had come up to him near the pitch.

"Thanks," he replied and made to move away.

"You don't recognise me, do you?"

Matthew looked at him. "Should I?"

"Hasn't your mother showed you any pictures of me?"

"Sorry, I don't talk to strangers," he said, a little puzzled by the question.

"Quite right too – but I'm your dad!"

Matthew was stunned. "Dad?"

His identity was confirmed when Matthew's mother came running across the pitch to reach them.

"What d'yer think you're doing?" she cried.

"Just speaking to our son. What's wrong with that?"

"Plenty! You've got no right to..."

"Course I have, woman. He's my son too."

"And a fat lot of interest you've shown in him all these years."

Their argument raged around Matthew, leaving him quite bewildered. "Stop it, b..both of you," he pleaded. "I just want to p..play footb..ball.

Dad stared at him. "Have you got a stutter?"

"See!" she exclaimed. "You didn't even know that, did you?"

Matthew left them to it and escaped to the safety of the changing area where Brad was sitting on one of the benches near a radiator.

"What's up, Matt? You look like you've just seen a ghost."

Matthew nodded, white-faced. "I have," he muttered, still shaking with the shock. "I've just m..met m..my dad."

"What's so bad about that?" he asked and then remembered that Matthew only lived with his mother. "Oh, yeah, right. Was it bad?"

Matthew pulled a face. "Not good."

"Right, come on back outside with me," the captain told him, standing up. "I know the best way to put that kind of stuff out of your mind. Let's go and kick a ball about and get ready for the Final."

Ups and Downs

The County Cup Final between Westgate and Kingston High School kicked off in front of the biggest crowd that the players had ever experienced. Besides families and friends, some of the other teams had also stayed to see who won the competition.

"Up the Kings!" cried a supporter. "Show this lot how to play football."

The Kings had every right to feel confident. They had won all their games that morning and scored lots of goals in the process. They passed the ball around so quickly and accurately, hardly allowing Westgate a kick, that Mr Blyton even counted the red shirts to check that both teams were playing seven-a-side.

"C'mon, the Magpies!" Ossie called out. "Get stuck in!"

"Magpies?" queried his brother. "Where's that name come from?"

"Their black and white kit, man," Ossie told him. "Good choice. You see – black and white can work real well together."

His nephew was the first 'Magpie' to respond. Josh won the ball with a crunching tackle in midfield and then swept it out to Matthew on the left wing. Sadly, for once, they did not seem to be on the same wavelength. Matthew wasn't expecting the pass and let the ball run under his boot and out of play.

"Oh, Matthew!" cried his mother. "Why did you go and do a silly thing like that?"

Matthew looked away, pretending that he hadn't heard.

"Are you Matthew's ma?" asked a woman standing next to her.

"What if I am?" she retorted. "Who are you?"

"Josh's ma. He's always talkin' 'bout your Matt. They're such good pals. Might be nice if we got to

know each other too. We seem to have one thing in common at least."

"What's that?"

"An ex-hubbie poppin' up again out the blue," said Mrs Williams and then smiled. "Sure we could both do without that."

Ms Jones smiled back at her. "I didn't mean to make a scene in front of people. I was just so mad."

"Don't worry 'bout it. I know how you feel."

They were so busy talking, neither of them saw the first goal. It was even doubtful whether Joe saw much of it. He hardly made a move as the ball sped by him and buried itself in the bottom corner of the net.

Brad was furious. The captain blamed himself for allowing the Kings' striker such a clear sight of goal.

"Should've got across to block the shot," he moaned. "I gave him far too much room."

"Not your fault," Anil admitted. "I'm the one supposed to be marking him."

"Never mind," shouted Mr Blyton. "It can't be helped. Let's go and look for that equalizer."

Josh almost found one too. Receiving the ball on the halfway line, he beat two opponents on a weaving, solo run towards goal before firing in a shot that grazed the top of the crossbar.

"That's the way, Joshie-Boy," cried Ossie. "You show 'em."

It was a rare moment of danger for the Kings. Leela found herself up against the best defender she had ever faced and was barely able to get a touch of the ball. As for Matthew, his mind was in so much of a mess, still brooding over his father's sudden appearance, that the match seemed to be passing him by.

"Wake up, Matt!" bellowed his dad when Matthew was easily robbed of the ball again. "Fight for it!"

Matthew shook his head, trying to clear it, but it was no use. He just wasn't in the mood for playing football.

Right on half-time, Joe had to repeat the job that all goalkeepers hate – fishing the ball out of his own net. He had made a valiant effort to save this shot, diving full-length to get his fingertips to the low, skidding ball, but he only managed to deflect it against the inside of the post on its way into the goal.

"Two-nil," Brad muttered as he trudged towards Mr Blyton for the brief break. "Don't look like I'm gonna get my hands on that cup now."

"Well at least we got to the Final," said Panna.

"Not enough," grunted the captain. "I wanted to win."

"There's still time to get back into this match," Mr Blyton told them, trying to sound more optimistic than he felt. "If we can score an early goal second half, you never know what might happen."

The teacher just had to hope for the best. There was little he could do to change things now. He already had his best players on the pitch, even if some of them were under-performing.

"C'mon, team, we can still do it," Josh urged as they took up their positions for the second half. "Goals win games!"

"That's m'boy!" Da laughed, grinning at his younger brother. "That's what I've kept tellin' both of you."

"Dead right too," Ossie grinned back. "Trouble is, man, sometimes the other lot go and score more goals than us!"

Josh also went up to Matthew to have a quiet word with him. "You OK?"

"Not really."

"Thought not. What's wrong?"

"Everything. M..my dad's here for a start."

"Sorry, Matt," Josh said, realising now why he was upset. "Must've been a bit of a shock, like."

Matthew nodded. "Sure was. I thought he was dead."

There was no chance to say anything else. The whistle blew, the Kings went straight on to the attack again and Josh chased after the ball to help out in defence. He was too late to do anything, but fortunately Joe had not been caught cold. The goalkeeper was alert to the danger and had the shot well covered, getting his body right behind the ball to gather it safely up into his arms.

Joe's long clearance was well controlled by Leela, who had the luxury of more space than she'd been allowed all match. She knew why that was, too. Her previous marker had been replaced by a substitute.

Must think they've got the match won already, she realised, moving forward with the ball at her feet. *Well, they can think again.*

Leela made the most of her newfound freedom. She took on and beat the substitute, pushing the ball through his legs, then her shot forced the Kings' goalie into making his first save of the game to concede a corner.

"Mark up!" cried the goalie, as Leela went over to take the kick.

The defenders failed to do their jobs properly. Leela's low cross somehow squeezed through a tangle of legs to reach Josh, standing unmarked on the far side of the area. He needed only two touches. One to control the ball and the second to steer it wide of the goalie into the net.

"Goal!" whooped Uncle Ossie. "Magic, Joshie-Boy!"

Westgate were now only 2-1 behind. But the Kings were good enough to weather the storm of the next few attacks – albeit with the help of a large slice of luck when a long-range effort from Brad thumped against the crossbar – and then claim their crown with a third strike of their own.

It was a cruel blow. Joe seemed to have the shot covered until the ball took a late deflection to veer away into the opposite side of the goal.

That was it. Try as they might, Westgate could not score again and the Kings were soon celebrating their deserved victory.

The Kings' captain led his team-mates forward to claim the cup and their medals from Ossie Williams, who would much rather have handed them over to Westgate School.

Uncle Ossie enjoyed his next duty far more.

He also presented an individual award, a silver statuette of a footballer, to his own nephew, who had been judged the Player of the Tournament. "Well done, Joshie-Boy! Hold it up high and smile for the cameras."

"Well done, everybody!" called out Mr Blyton over the applause as each member of the squad went up in turn to receive their runners-up medal.

As a disappointed Matthew stuffed his medal into a coat pocket without even looking at it, he felt a tap on his shoulder.

"Hard luck, son," said his dad. "Not your day in the end, I'm afraid."

Matthew shook his head. "No, it wasn't," he agreed.

"But at least one good thing's come out of it," Dad said. "We've found each other again. Let's make sure we keep in touch in future."

Matthew made no reply. He was still too confused to know what to say.

He was rescued by Josh. "C'mon, Matt!" he cried, dragging him away by the arm. "Uncle Ossie's gonna treat us both to monster burgers."

Matthew hesitated. "Er..I'll have to check with M..mam first."

"Da's already done that," Josh told him. "It's OK so long as they bring us straight home after."

The two mothers had their own plans for lunch. "Why don't you come back to my place?" suggested Josh's mother. "We can have a bite to eat and a coffee."

"Thanks – I'd like that," Matthew's mother said with a smile. "Let's slip away while nobody's looking."

They went off together arm in arm, giggling, while the boys jumped into the back of Ossie's car.

"Can't be bad, this, eh?" Josh grinned. "Even if we did lose the final."

"Yeah, you can't win 'em all, as they say," Matthew replied with a shrug.

"Guess so," Josh said, gazing at the statuette. "As long as we win some."

"Dead right, Joshie-Boy," Ossie chuckled. "There's always another game."

Author's note

Good advice for writers is to write about
what you know. Well, one of the things
I know something about is football, as a fan,
player and coach. Lots of my soccer stories
seem to involve goalkeepers as main characters –
perhaps because I was a keeper in my
younger days. Sadly, a keeper can go from hero
to zero just by making a single mistake.
Hope you have enjoyed this colourful
soccer story, even if it is in black and white!

Also available from
Frances Lincoln Children's Books

BUTTER-FINGER
Bob Cattell and John Agard
Illustrated by Pam Smy

Riccardo Small may not be a great cricketer – he's only
played twice before for Calypso Cricket Club – but he's
mad about the game and can tell you the averages of every
West Indies cricketer in history. His other love is
writing calypsos. Today is Riccardo's chance to make his
mark with Calypso CC against The Saints. The game goes
right down to the wire with captain, Natty and team-mates,
Bashy and Leo striving for victory, but then comes the
moment that changes everything for Riccardo...

ISBN 978-1-84507-376-3

SHINE ON, BUTTERFINGER

Bob Cattell and John Agard

Illustrated by Pam Smy

Calypso and cricket come together in the Island's Carnival, and Riccardo has to choose between his two passions. He has been invited to sing at the annual Calypso Final, competing against the most famous singers on the Island, and amidst the pan bands, the masqueraders and the stick-fighters he discovers why the singing competition is called 'Calypso War'. Meanwhile his team-mates at Calypso Cricket Club are playing the most important game in their history and their new captain, Bashy has a lot to learn in a very short time…

ISBN 978-1-84507-626-9

ROAR, BULL, ROAR!

Andrew Fusek Peters and Polly Peters

Illustrated by Anke Weckmann

What is the real story of the ghostly Roaring Bull?
Who is the batty old lady in the tattered clothes?
Why is the new landlord such a nasty piece of work?
Czech brother and sister Jan and Marie arrive in rural
England in the middle of the night – and not everyone is
welcoming. As they try to settle into their new school,
they are plunged into a series of mysteries. Old legends
are revived as Jan and Marie unearth shady secrets in
a desperate bid to save their family from eviction.
In their quest, they find unlikely allies and deadly enemies –
who will stop at nothing to keep the past buried.

ISBN 978-1-84507-520-0

FALCON'S FURY

Andrew Fusek Peters and Polly Peters

Illustrated by Naomi Tipping

Hidden treasure … a secret crime … the precious eggs
of a bird of prey… When Jan and Marie discover who is
stealing and selling the eggs of a peregrine falcon,
they suddenly find themselves in danger. Only the ancient
legend of Stokey Castle can help them – and the falcon
will show them the way.
Andrew Fusek Peters' and Polly Peters' exciting new novel
revisits the Klecheks, a family from the Czech Republic
newly settled in Shropshire. Teenage brother and sister
Jan and Marie are soon unravelling villainy and mysteries,
but they will need even greater courage and ingenuity
to face what is about to happen.

ISBN: 978-1-84507-634-4

CHRISTOPHE'S STORY

Nicki Cornwell

Illustrated by Karin Littlewood

Christophe has a story inside him – and this story
wants to be told. But with a new country, a new school
and a new language to cope with, Christophe can't find
the right words. He wants to tell the whole school
about why he had to leave Rwanda, why he has a bullet
wound on his chest and what happened to his baby brother,
but has he got the courage to be a storyteller?
Christophe must find a way to break through all
these barriers, so he can share his story with everyone.

ISBN 978-1-84507-521-7

WASIM THE WANDERER

Chris Ashley

Illustrated by Kate Pankhurst

No one at school can score a goal like Wasim!
So he is trying out his football skills for
Teamwork 10,000 and that might just lead to a trial
with the Woodley Wanderers! But how can he play
his best football with Robert Bailey lurking around
every corner – and then on the football pitch too?

ISBN 978-1-84507-776-1

Also by Chris Ashley: Wasim One-Star